Baxter Turns Down His Buzz

A Story for Little Kids About ADHD

by James M. Foley, DEd

illustrated by
Shirley Ng-Benitez

Magination Press • Washington, DC • American Psychological Association

To Beth, wife, mother, and teacher who helped many Baxters turn down their buzz—*JMF*

For my daughters, Sierra and Noëlle, with love, and for those whom this book touches—*SN-B*

Published by
MAGINATION PRESS®
An Educational Publishing Foundation Book
American Psychological Association
750 First Street NE
Washington, DC 20002

Magination Press is a registered trademark of the American Psychological Association.

For more information about our books, including a complete catalog, please write to us, call 1-800-374-2721, or visit our website at www.apa.org/pubs/magination.

Book design by Gwen Grafft
Printed by Phoenix Color Corporation, Hagerstown, MD

Library of Congress Cataloging-in-Publication Data
Names: Foley, James M., 1947– | Ng-Benitez, Shirley, illustrator.
Title: Baxter turns down his buzz : a story for little kids about ADHD / by James M. Foley, DEd ;
    illustrated by Shirley Ng-Benitez.
Description: Washington, DC : Magination Press, 2016. | "American Psychological Association." |
    Summary: "A high-energy rabbit that must learn to control his activity level and
    impulsiveness. Baxter's uncle Barnaby guides Baxter through
    the steps necessary to 'turn down his buzz.' Techniques
    such as mindfulness, progressive relaxation, and
    visualization are employed"— Provided by publisher.
Identifiers: LCCN 2016005294 |
    ISBN 9781433822681 (hardcover) |
    ISBN 1433822687 (hardcover)
Subjects: | CYAC: Attention-deficit hyperactivity
    disorder—Fiction. | Relaxation—Fiction. |
    Rabbits—Fiction. | Forest animals—Fiction.
Classification: LCC PZ7.1.F65 Bax 2016 |
    DDC [E]—dc23 LC record available at
    http://lccn.loc.gov/2016005294

Manufactured in the United States of America
10 9 8 7 6 5 4 3 2 1

Baxter was the fastest bunny in the forest.

His mind buzzed with thoughts and his body wanted to zoom.

First, he would tap his little
bunny foot on the ground. Then
he would shake his tail, wiggle
his ears, and *zooooom,* he was off!

He whizzed past the weasels
and dashed past the deer.

He was one quick
and smart little rabbit.

One day, Baxter's uncle Barnaby noticed Baxter
sitting under a tree, not zooming around like usual.

"What's wrong with my little Baxter?" said Uncle Barnaby.

"I have no friends," said Baxter. "None of the other forest animals like me. I don't get it. I am the first to win the forest games. I am the first one to finish any forest work."

"Baxter, I have watched you closely over the years.
I even saw the day that you won the annual forest race."

"Oh yeah, I was really fast and beat everyone
to the finish line," said Baxter.

"Well, do you remember barging into the badgers
and ramming into the raccoons on the race track?"

"Nope," replied Baxter.

"Do you remember grabbing all the water bottles
at the end of the race?"

"Oh yeah, I was really thirsty. The other animals
were mad because I didn't share."

"Baxter, we rabbits are fast and smart.
We see so far and run so fast that we often
zoom right by the other forest creatures.

Zooming is usually a good thing, like when you are
in a race and want to win. But sometimes you can
lose control of your zoom, like when you rammed
into the raccoons in last year's forest race.

My little nephew, to be happy you must learn
the lesson that all rabbits must learn. You must
learn to turn down your buzz and control your zoom!"

"But Uncle Barnaby, how can I turn down my buzz?"

"Well, Baxter, your buzz starts in your head, right between
those bunny ears. You must slow down your thoughts
and be aware of what is happening around you.

Once you have turned down your buzz,
you can relax your body and control your zoom."

"Baxter, listen and I will tell you what is happening for
old Barnaby, RIGHT NOW! I feel a breeze gently
touching my fur. I can smell the new spring flowers.
Mr. Squirrel is chattering at Mrs. Squirrel high up in this tree."

"Now it's your turn. Close your eyes. What do you hear?"

"Well, I can hear Mr. Jay squawking in the tree,
and Mr. Frog croaking in the stream."

"Good, Baxter. Just…listen."

"Now, what do you feel?"

"I feel the wind in my fur and the grass tickling my feet."

"Good, just…feel."

"What do you smell?"

"I smell the sweet carrots growing in Mr. Bear's garden."

"Okay, just…smell.

Now, breathe in the smell of the carrots and then
breathe out. Keep breathing slowly in through
your nose and out through your mouth as I talk."

"Now, Baxter, keep your eyes closed and put a picture of race day in your head. Do you see the picture?"

"Yeah, Uncle Barnaby, I am standing at the starting line right beside Ralphie Raccoon!"

"Good! Now we are going to work on relaxing your body to control your zoom."

"Feel your foot start to tap on the ground. It wants
to go fast, but squeeze it tight while I count
one…two…three…four…five…and now relax your foot."

"Feel your tail start to twitch and then squeeze
your body from your tail to your foot while I count
one…two…three…four…five…and then relax."

"Then feel your ears begin to wiggle and
squeeze your whole body while I count
one…two…three…four…five…and then relax."

"Okay, Baxter, open your eyes. Now I want you to practice
paying attention to what is going on around you.
Then, practice relaxing your whole body.
On the day of the big race, you will be able to
pay attention to the race track and all the other animals."

Day after day Baxter practiced turning down the buzz in his head
and controlling his zoom just the way Barnaby had shown him.

Finally it was race day. Chester the Owl, the Forest Mayor,
was about to start the race. Baxter stepped to the
starting line. He closed his eyes and took a deep breath.

Baxter heard the birds in the trees and felt the wind in his fur.
He could smell the pine trees up ahead.

When he felt his foot start to tap, he squeezed his foot, then relaxed it.
Baxter relaxed his tail, then his ears, then his whole body.

As Baxter opened his eyes, Chester waved the starting flag.
Zooooom, off went Baxter.

Just as Baxter flew around the first curve, Ralphie Raccoon
fell right in front of him. Baxter skidded to a stop.
He picked up Ralphie, dusted him off, and zoomed ahead.

Baxter sped away from all the other animals. As he got close
to the finish line, a baby chipmunk crawled out onto the race track!
Baxter slowed just enough to scoop up the chipmunk.

He zoomed across the finish line with the
chipmunk in his arms, just in time to win the race!

"Thank you for saving baby Chippy!" said Mrs. Chipper.

"Way to go, Baxter!" said Barnaby. "You won the race,
AND you did a great job paying attention!"

"Thanks, Uncle Barnaby," said Baxter. "I guess my buzz is just right!"

Note to Parents and Caregivers

Every child can benefit from learning strategies that teach them to be more mindful of their surroundings and to regulate their behavior. Children who have been diagnosed with attention-deficit/hyperactivity disorder (ADHD) may especially benefit from learning these skills.

ADHD is a neurodevelopmental condition which can be present at an early age and is seen across home, school, and community settings. The core characteristics of ADHD are behaviors associated with symptoms such as inattentiveness, hyperactivity, impulsiveness, and difficulty with organization and planning. Most young children demonstrate normal activity and curiosity, particularly during the preschool years. When your child's activity level and impulsivity are extreme, difficult to manage, and persistent, it may indicate ADHD. If you observe such behaviors in your child, it is important to contact a professional competent in the diagnosis of ADHD. A visit with your child's pediatrician is a good place to start.

The good news is that living with ADHD can be managed through treatment. The components of treatment often include psychotherapy or counseling for the child and/or parent, behavioral management strategies for the family, and medication prescribed and monitored by a physician. In therapy, parents learn strategies to support their child and children learn skills to manage their behavior. As Baxter did in the story, your child can learn skills to help "turn down their buzz" or "slow down their zoom."

HOW THIS BOOK CAN HELP

Baxter Turns Down His Buzz is the story of a high-energy rabbit who must learn to control his activity level and impulsiveness. Baxter's uncle Barnaby guides Baxter through the steps necessary to "turn down his buzz." Techniques such as mindfulness and progressive relaxation are portrayed in the story. A young child who is able to relate to the animal characters can imitate their coping strategies with direction from their parent.

The bedtime story presents a precious opportunity for children and parents to communicate and review the day. Managing a child's impulsive behavior often leads to limit setting and stress. Reading *Baxter Turns Down His Buzz* presents an opportunity for the parent and child to review helpful strategies, end the day on a positive note, and make plans for a better tomorrow.

HOW TO HELP YOUR CHILD REGULATE THEIR BEHAVIOR

Children with ADHD, like all children, benefit from having their parents' love, attention, and support. The following are some suggestions for helping your child manage their behavior while maintaining a positive and loving relationship with your child.

Communicate. Establish regular rituals that provide the opportunity for an open dialogue with your child. The ideal time to interact with your child may be at bedtime while reading a story in your child's room, when your child is comfortable in his or her own bed surrounded by familiar stuffed animals. You may also find time for regular talks around the dinner table or in the car on the way home from school. Whenever you talk with your child, give your child your full attention. Correcting or managing your child's impulsive behavior may at times cause hurt feelings and your child's behavior may challenge and frustrate you. Carving out one-on-one time to communicate is important for maintaining a positive and loving relationship.

Focus on your child's strengths. Highlight the qualities that make your child unique, such as their curiosity, humor, and insight. Perhaps your child has channeled their energy into athletics or art and would appreciate your recognition of their efforts. Tell your child that together you will learn some skills to help them with all the things that they do well. The skills can also be used to help them handle more difficult situations.

Teach the skills used by Baxter to turn down his buzz. In the story, Baxter's uncle Barnaby teaches Baxter the skills of mindfulness and progressive relaxation. You can help your child learn these skills as well by using modeling, practice, and reinforcement.

Mindfulness is directing our attention to the present. At the simplest level, it is being aware of our breathing and sensory experience.

- Modeling: Find a quiet place and sit with your child. Close your eyes, breathe gently in through your nose and out through your mouth. Slowly and quietly describe what you hear, feel, and smell, just as Barnaby did in the story. Have your child do the same.

- Practice: Periodically, throughout the day, take a few minutes to practice the exercise with your child.

- Reinforcement: Give praise and encouragement for your child's efforts at learning the skills. Give special recognition if the child independently practices the skill.

Progressive relaxation is the process of relaxing the muscles of the body. The method used by Baxter is to tighten the muscles for a matter of seconds then to release and relax them.

- Modeling: Read the section of the story that describes Barnaby's instructions to Baxter on relaxing his body. Demonstrate the relaxation with one of your child's stuffed animals. After demonstrating, gently shake the stuffed animal and say, "See how relaxed and floppy your stuffed animal is? Now show me with your body how relaxed and floppy your stuffed animal is." It is best to use this method of relaxation with preschool youngsters rather than a formal step-by-step method of muscle relaxation. If your child is older, it is best to consult his psychotherapist on a preferred method of progressive relaxation.

- Practice: Find time during the day to practice the skill. When the child seems ready, try practicing both mindfulness and relaxation when they need to turn down their buzz.

- Reinforcement: Again, give praise and encouragement to your child's efforts at learning the skills. Give special recognition if the child independently practices the skill.

Apply the skills. The first step is to identify the situations in which your child needs to apply their new skills in order to regulate their behavior. At any age, it is crucial that your child feel like they are a partner in the process and that learning the skill is a positive step rather than a negative one. It is helpful to begin the discussion by listing all the positive aspects of your child's active behavior. For example, maybe your child is good at finding items in a store, helping you out with daily activities, or noticing new aspects of their environment.

With your child's participation, choose a situation in which to apply the new skills. Your choice should be one that has the greatest chance of success for your child and that allows you to control the situation (e.g. your child helping you load the family washing machine). Here are the steps in the process.

Practice mindfulness. Within the immediate area, guide your child in the mindfulness exercise.

Practice relaxation. Guide your child through the relaxation exercise.

Visualize success. Just as Baxter closed his eyes and visualized being successful in the race, have your child close their eyes and guide them through the steps of helping mom or dad successfully load the washing machine.

Use reinforcement. Provide praise and encouragement throughout the exercise when appropriate. As a parent, your attention and genuine encouragement is the most powerful incentive for your child. When learning skills that are difficult for an active child, however, a reinforcement system (e.g., a sticker chart) can be very helpful as well. Reinforce your child's progress using a point system (or chips, marbles, or stickers). Sit with your child and list reasonable rewards which can be purchased with a set number of points, chips, marbles, or stickers (depending on the age of the child). For example, your child could be allowed to choose what the family has for dinner, from a set of options. As your child practices the skill, provide encouragement and feedback on the amount of chips that they have earned.

Helping your child "turn down their buzz" is not an easy task, but don't be discouraged. It is important to use all the resources available to you to ensure success. Do not be afraid to seek professional help. Many children with ADHD benefit from psychotherapy and medication. If your child has been diagnosed with ADHD, seek at least a consultation with a licensed mental health professional to determine if psychotherapy or medication may be helpful for your child. In addition, you can seek extra help and support for specific areas of your child's life. Tutors, school counselors, and support groups are all great resources.

Children with ADHD often have active parents who may or may not have been given an official diagnosis of ADHD. If this describes you, it is important not to blame yourself for your child's difficulties. Focus on the benefits that your alertness and energy level have provided for you. See yourself as a consultant with the hard earned knowledge needed to guide your child towards a positive life path. Therapy can be incredibly helpful for parents as well, and can give you the skills to work with your child and support their success.

About the Author

James M. Foley, DEd, is a licensed psychologist who has recently retired from his private practice in Maine. He has served as a clinical director and member of a community mental health center children's service team and has extensive experience as a school psychologist and child and family therapist. He now resides in Sonoma County, CA, in close proximity to his two adult children, and serves as psychological consultant to a local school district.

About the Illustrator

Shirley Ng-Benitez loves to draw! Nature, family, and fond memories of her youth inspire her mixed media illustrations. Since '98, she's owned gabbyandco.com, designing, illustrating, and handlettering for the technology, greeting card, medical, toy, and publishing industries. She's living her dream, illustrating and writing picture books in San Martin, CA, with her husband and two daughters. Shirley is honored to have illustrated this book as well as *Danny and the Blue Cloud,* also written by Dr. James M. Foley and published by Magination Press. You can find more of her work on her website, www.shirleyngbenitez.com.

About Magination Press

Magination Press is an imprint of the American Psychological Association, the largest scientific and professional organization representing psychologists in the United States and the largest association of psychologists worldwide.